TOW TRUCK JOE

June Sobel   *illustrated by* Patrick Corrigan

Houghton Mifflin Harcourt

Boston   New York

Text written by June Sobel
Illustrations created by Patrick Corrigan
Jacket and title page lettering created by José Bernabé

hmhbooks.com

The art was drawn with pencil and colored digitally.
The type was set in Bookman ITC and Schuss Hand ITC.

ISBN: 978-0-358-05312-5

Manufactured in China
SCP 10 9 8 7 6 5 4 3 2 1
4500760868

BIG WHEEL COOKI
THEY TASTE
WHEELY GREAT
BIG

KNEAD FOR SPEED BAKERY

e Engine Room

ROADSTER DONUTS

DRIVE-THRU

Joe the Tow is on the go.
All day long, he honks, "Hello!"

A fix-it truck for small and large
tows cars and trucks to his garage.

Patch, his pup, sniffs out trouble
so Joe can help out on the double.

Driving up and down the street,
Joe sees cars and trucks to greet.

GARAGE D'OR
JEWELRY

CENTRAL CAR PARK

A cement mixer passes by.
Joe the Tow beep-beeps, "Hi!"

The cookie cart is in a rush
but stuck inside the traffic crush.

Red light. **STOP!** Green light. **GO!**
Joe moves on and honks, "Hello!"

Patch the Pup cries out a yelp.
"That car won't start! Joe can help!"

Tow truck arrives before too long.
Patch lifts the hood to see what's wrong.

"Joe can fix it! He is able!"
Joe connects his jumper cable!

Car engine hums a happy song.
The fix-it tow truck moves along.

ATTACK
OF THE 50 FT.
CAR

NIGHT OF
THE LIVING
PARKING
METER

DRIVE-I

MONSTER TRUCKS

01

The fire engine's sirens yell!
The ice cream truck rings its bell.

The milk truck is running late.
The grocery truck cannot wait.

Red light. STOP! Green light. GO!
Joe moves on and honks, "Hello!"

Patch the Pup cries out a yelp
"A tire's flat! Joe can help!"

The mail truck's tire is out of air.
Joe the Tow has a spare.

The wheel is fixed and spins around
when Joe the Tow hears a sound!

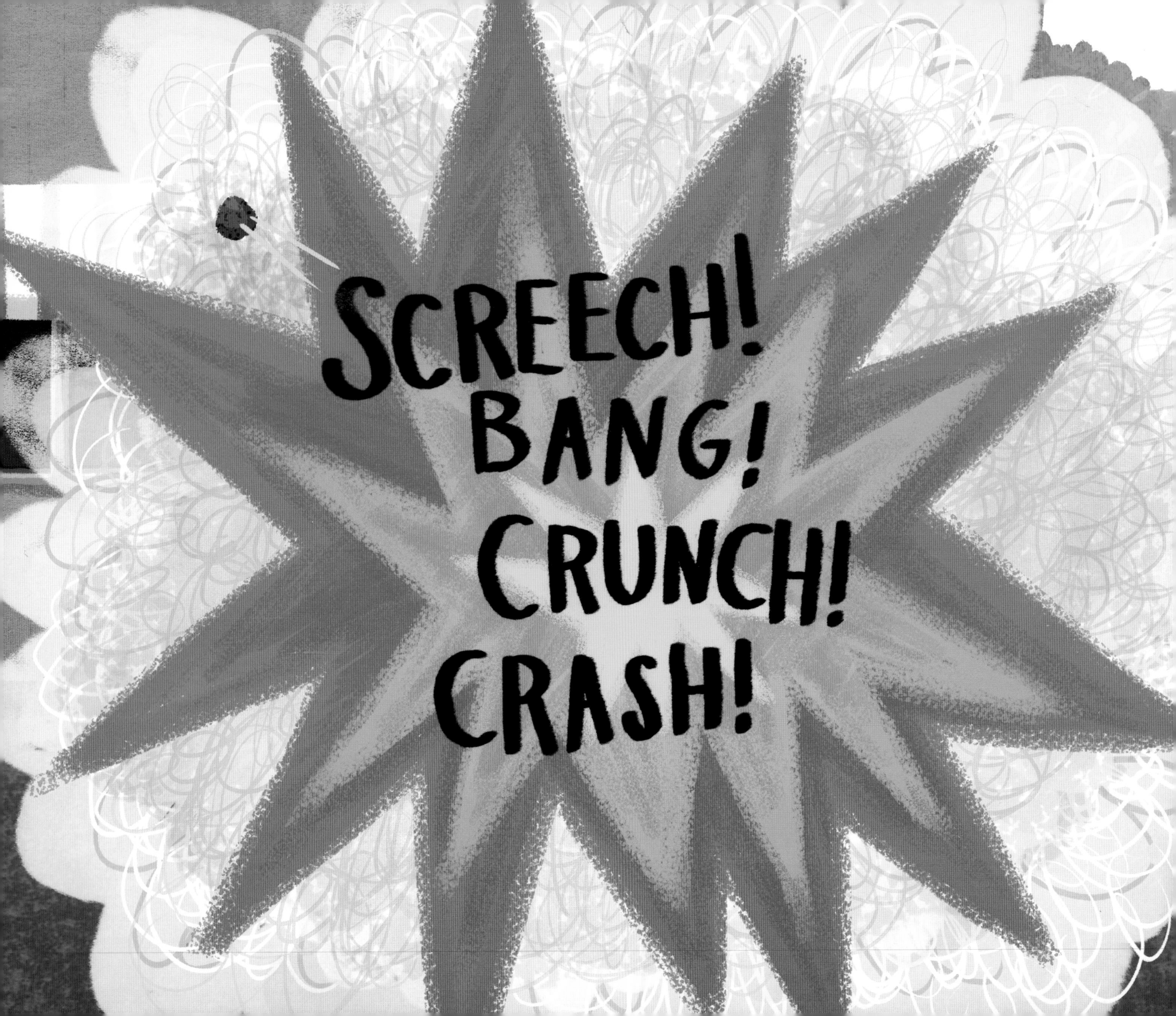
SCREECH!
BANG!
CRUNCH!
CRASH!

Joe races over in a flash!

The milk truck sped. A cart was struck.
Full of cookies! What bad luck!

All the cookies now are crushed!
Just because the milk truck rushed!

Cookie crumb piles fill the road.

Engines grumble. Traffic slowed.

Joe honks to take time out.
No trucks beep. No trucks pout.

ONE for all! **ALL** for one!
We can fix it! Let's have fun!

~TRENDY A-TIRE~

Joe and friends act with haste.
No cookie crumbs will go to waste!

The grocery truck knows what to bring.
Sugar and vanilla—just the thing!

Patch the Pup, always a fixer,
pours some milk into the mixer.

The mixer stirs round and round.
Trucks all watch without a sound.

The ice cream truck's bell rings twice.
Her freezer's empty and cold as ice.

~TRENDY A-T

Patch sniffs and licks. It's not a dream.
It's Cookie Crunch—their new ice cream!

Trucks all follow Patch and Joe,
driving carefully, going slow!

The Engine Room

OIL

01 FIRE DEPT

DRIV

A busy day comes to an end
for Joe the Tow, a good friend!